I0572414

Published by: Camistin Publishing

Camistin Publishing books are available anywhere books are available anywhere books are sold. Substantial discounts are available on bulk quantities to corporations, educational institutions, professional associations, and other organizations. Requests for support, reproduction and bulk sales may be made via email to support@camistin.com.

Paperback ISBN: 978-1-62408-015-9
eBook ISBN: 978-1-62408-016-6

Thank you for supporting Camistin Publishing, a veteran owned small business.

Ye Are Gods…

*Human Religion Unveiled –
An Alien's Cosmic Quest for
Eternal Truth*

By Vega Sparx

Introduction: A Cosmic Quest for Truth

Greetings once again, Earth friends! My first adventure into decoding the essence of Earth's most mysterious gender was both instructive and revealing. While a very small minority threatened me with elimination for my home planet's understanding of eternal gender identity, most have embraced my quest to understand the human race with open minds and hearts. Now, I find myself drawn into yet another fascinating, profound, and deeply unifying yet sometimes dividing concept: religion.

Your art, your music, your very history—so much of it is intertwined with your yearning for something greater than yourselves. It's beautiful, baffling, and, as I've come to learn, profoundly human. The friends I met under the streets of Vegas would often use the word "God." At first, I thought it was merely an expression of sadness or frustration.

Then I encountered two young men dressed in bright white shirts with a curious strip of fabric tied around their necks—"ties," I later discovered. Their black name tags displayed their names and a reference to someone called Jesus Christ. They informed me they had a message from God. Naturally, my curiosity was piqued! It was my first step toward understanding that God—and the many other names humanity uses for the Creator—holds immense significance across your world.

From the moment I became a native of Las Vegas, Nevada, I couldn't help but notice humanity's fascination with the divine. Your places of worship, whether grand cathedrals or humble prayer rooms, dot the landscapes of your cities and towns. By chance, I stumbled upon one of my favorite buildings in Las Vegas—the large temple on Sunrise Mountain to the east. I spent several nights sleeping in a nearby cave, and each morning I would walk through its meticulously cared-for gardens. The beauty and tranquility of the grounds filled me with a profound sense of peace, as though I were standing on truly sacred ground.

On my home planet, religion and spirituality aren't so enigmatic. While there are some variations in beliefs and practices, we live with a clear understanding of our eternal identities, our purpose, and our connection to the cosmos. Our spiritual understandings are deeply unified—few competing doctrines, few debates over sacred texts. Yet here on Earth, you have a myriad of religions, each with its own traditions, beliefs, and practices. How does one species arrive at so many paths to the same truths? And what do these paths reveal about you—and perhaps even about me?

My mission for this book is simple yet ambitious: to explore Earth's religions with curiosity and respect, to uncover the eternal truths they share, and to seek unity in the pursuit of truth. Along the way, I'll also compare these findings with the spiritual understanding of my home planet, sharing insights that might astonish you, challenge you, or even leave you laughing at my (frequent) missteps.

Religion is deeply personal, and sometimes, discussing it feels a bit like walking through a field of your Earth cacti—one wrong step, and ouch! My goal isn't to critique or diminish but to learn and celebrate the truths that bring you closer to the divine. After all, truth, regardless of its perceived source, belongs to everyone.

This journey will take us across your continents and centuries of mortal time, diving into the practices and beliefs of some of the world's major religions. We'll explore sacred and holy days, fasting, the significance of prophets and revelation, the mysteries of the soul's eternal journey, and the divine potential that resides within every human. Along the way, I'll share my thoughts, my discoveries, and, of course, my alien perspective on what it all means.

Expect moments of awe, moments of confusion, and, undoubtedly, moments where I unintentionally make a fool of myself—like the time I mistook a prayer rug for a decorative wall hanging (but more on that later).

So, dear reader, whether you're a seeker of truth, a devoted believer, or simply curious about how an alien views human spirituality, I invite you to join me on this cosmic quest. Together, let's uncover the truths that unite us, celebrate the diversity that enriches us, and find common ground in our shared humanity.

Are you ready to embark on this interfaith journey with me? Buckle up—this one might just take us beyond the stars.

Chapter 1: Hinduism - The Cosmic Dance of Life

Inhabitants of Earth! On my home planet, cosmic truth and enlightenment is a central theme—a harmonious rhythm that connects all life. As I began my exploration of Earth's religions, I found a profound resonance with this idea in Hinduism, where the dance of existence takes center stage.

My journey began at the vibrant Hindu and Jain temple in Las Vegas. The temple stood as a spiritual beacon amid the city's neon brilliance—a testament to the sacred existing alongside the worldly. Priya, a friend I'd met at a local Indian restaurant (where I discovered the culinary wonder of dosas!), kindly invited me to learn more about her faith.

"This is more than a religion, Vega," Priya said as we entered the temple's fragrant, colorful embrace. "Hinduism is a way of life. It's how we connect with the universe."

Her words intrigued me. "Where do I start?" I asked.

I marveled at her words and asked, "Where do I start?"

"Start with the Bhagavad Gita," she said, handing me a copy of the text. "It's the essence of our teachings."

The Bhagavad Gita, or the "Song of the Lord," is a conversation between the warrior Arjuna and the god Krishna, who serves as his charioteer. As I read, one passage leaped out at me:

"You have the right to perform your prescribed duties, but you are not entitled to the

fruits of your actions. Never consider yourself the cause of the results of your activities, and never be attached to not doing your duty." (Bhagavad Gita 2.47)

I paused, struck by the depth of this teaching. "Priya, does this mean humans should act without expecting rewards or anything in return?"

She nodded. "Yes, Vega. It's about focusing on your dharma—your life's duty or your path in life—without attachment to the outcome. This detachment liberates us from suffering."

I reflected on my own actions since arriving on Earth. Have I been too fixated on finding a way home? Perhaps embracing my mission without clinging to the results could bring me a sense of peace.

The Gita also spoke of karma, the universal law of cause and effect. Another passage stood out:

"As a man casts off worn-out garments and takes new ones, so the soul casts off its worn-out

body and enters others that are new." (Bhagavad Gita 2.22)

This idea of reincarnation intrigued me. On my planet, we understand the eternal nature of the soul, but the concept of rebirth in new forms offered a fascinating perspective. The soul, it seemed, was on an eternal journey, learning and evolving with each new life. On my planet we do believe in the spirit does cast off its worn-out body through death and that it enters a new body, but the new one is a perfected version of the old. And thus we continue in the eternities and an immortal perfected entity fashioned after the image of God.

Priya invited me to accompany her to the temple for a morning puja (prayer ritual). As we entered the sacred space, I was overwhelmed by its vibrant energy. Flowers adorned statues of deities, candles flickered, and devotees sang hymns with heartfelt devotion.

"This is Krishna," Priya said, pointing to a beautifully adorned statue. "He teaches us about love and devotion."

During the ceremony, I noticed how every action—offering flowers, lighting lamps, ringing bells—was performed with reverence. I asked Priya about the significance.

"These rituals connect us to the divine," she explained. "They remind us that the sacred is present in all things, even in the smallest act."

The idea resonated deeply. Could it be that divinity exists even in my alien missteps? I recalled spilling water at the temple entrance and accidentally blessing my shoes. The devotees found it amusing and said Krishna must have a sense of humor. A comforting thought!

I marveled at the idea that divinity could be found everywhere. It was a reminder that even my journey on Earth, with its challenges and surprises, was part of a larger, sacred tapestry.

As I sat in the temple courtyard, I reflected on the profound truths I had encountered. Hinduism, with its focus on dharma, karma, and moksha (liberation), offered a framework for navigating life's complexities with purpose and grace.

I couldn't help but think of another passage from the Gita:

"When a man has freed himself from attachment to the results of work, and from desires for the enjoyment of sense objects, he ascends to the highest perfection that can be attained by renunciation." (Bhagavad Gita 18.49)

Was this the secret to inner peace—not just for humans but for all beings across the cosmos? Perhaps embracing this teaching could help me find balance in my own journey.

Hinduism had shown me that life is not a linear path but a cosmic dance, where every step, no matter how small, is part of a greater rhythm. The divine is in the details, the actions, and the very essence of existence.

With gratitude, I thanked Priya and promised to carry these lessons with me as I continued my exploration of Earth's religions. Hinduism had set the stage for this cosmic quest, offering wisdom that transcended cultural and planetary boundaries.

As I departed, Priya placed a small flower in my hand. "May your journey be blessed, Vega," she said.

Next, I would explore another tradition—each step of this journey bringing me closer to understanding the unity that underpins the diversity of Earth's beliefs. What truths would I uncover next? Only time—and perhaps a few more adventures—would tell.

Chapter 2: Buddhism - The Path to Enlightenment

If Hinduism is a cosmic dance, then Buddhism feels like the quiet pause between steps—a serene space for reflection, mindfulness, and seeking enlightenment. My exploration of Buddhism began, like many of my Earth adventures, in an unexpected place: a modest Buddhist center nestled in the heart of Las Vegas. Amid the city's glitz and neon chaos, this peaceful sanctuary felt like stepping into another dimension.

The Four Noble Truths: Understanding Suffering

The center's walls were adorned with serene Buddha statues and calming imagery of lotus flowers. I was welcomed by a kind monk named Bhante Tenzin, whose orange robe and gentle demeanor radiated calm.

"Vega," he began, He knew I was coming because I called before hand. But, it would have been pretty amazing if I was greeted by name by a chance walk in. "Buddhism teaches us to understand the nature of suffering and to walk the path toward enlightenment."

"Suffering?" I asked. "You mean like when I mistook a cactus for a chair? That was quite uncomfortable." Didn't really happen, but I thought I'd try to lighten my nerves with a joke.

He chuckled softly. "That too, but suffering—dukkha—goes deeper. It's the dissatisfaction we feel in life, the craving for things to be different."

He handed me a booklet outlining the Four Noble Truths, the cornerstone of Buddhist teachings:

1. The truth of suffering (dukkha): Life is marked by suffering.
2. The truth of the origin of suffering (samudaya): Suffering arises from craving and attachment.
3. The truth of the cessation of suffering (nirodha): Suffering can be overcome by letting go of craving.
4. The truth of the path (magga): The Eightfold Path leads to the cessation of suffering.

I pondered this. "So, humans suffer because they crave things?"

"Yes," Bhante replied. "Craving leads to attachment, and attachment leads to suffering. By letting go, we find peace."

Exploring the Eightfold Path

To better understand the way out of suffering, Bhante introduced me to the Eightfold Path, a practical guide for living which I would like to share with you. Perhaps it will help you along your path to truth:

1. Right View
2. Right Intention
3. Right Speech
4. Right Action
5. Right Livelihood
6. Right Effort
7. Right Mindfulness
8. Right Concentration

"Think of it as a roadmap," he said. "Each step brings us closer to enlightenment."

I found "Right Intention" particularly intriguing. "Does this mean humans must always have noble motives?" I asked.

"Exactly," Bhante replied. "Our intentions shape our actions, and our actions shape our lives."

This resonated with me. On my home planet, we have a similar principle: clarity of purpose guides harmonious living. Perhaps humans and my race aren't so different after all.

Bhante invited me to join a meditation session. The room was simple yet serene, filled with the scent of sandalwood incense. Participants sat cross-legged on cushions, their eyes gently closed.

"Focus on your breath," Bhante instructed. "Be present in this moment."

As I attempted to focus, my mind wandered. Should I try meditating standing up? What's for lunch? Does my translator work during deep breathing? It was harder than it looked.

"Be patient with yourself, Vega," Bhante said, noticing my fidgeting. "Mindfulness takes practice."

Eventually, I felt a moment of stillness—a brief pause where my thoughts quieted, and I simply existed. It was both humbling and profound.

Afterward, I asked Bhante, "Why is mindfulness so important?"

"Mindfulness helps us see things as they truly are," he explained. "It frees us from clinging to the past or worrying about the future."

This idea of living fully in the present struck a chord with me. Since arriving on Earth, I'd often been consumed by the desire to return home. Perhaps mindfulness could help me embrace my journey, wherever it leads.

Later, Bhante and I sat in the center's garden, shaded by a sprawling Bodhi tree. He shared the story of the Buddha, who renounced his royal life to seek enlightenment.

"Buddha taught us that attachment is the root of suffering," Bhante said. "By letting go, we find freedom."

I reflected on this. Could I let go of my attachment to finding a way back to my planet? It was a daunting thought, yet the idea of inner peace was appealing.

I asked Bhante, "Does letting go mean giving up on goals?"

"Not at all," he replied. "It means pursuing goals without being enslaved by the outcome. Non-attachment is freedom, not indifference."

This reminded me of the Bhagavad Gita's teaching on performing duties without attachment to results. Earth's wisdom seemed to echo across its religions.

As I left the Buddhist center, I felt a sense of calm and clarity. The Four Noble Truths and the Eightfold Path offered profound insights into the human condition—and perhaps even the universal condition.

Buddhism had taught me that suffering is a shared experience, but so is the potential for liberation. By embracing mindfulness, right intentions, and non-attachment, humans—and perhaps aliens—can find peace.

I couldn't help but recall Bhante's words: "The path to enlightenment begins with a single breath."

As I walked through the bustling streets of Las Vegas, I found myself breathing deeply, each step a small act of mindfulness. Buddhism had shown me a new way of being—a reminder that even in the midst of chaos, peace is possible.

Chapter 3: Judaism - A Covenant Path with the Divine

On my journey through the rich tapestry of human spirituality, I've often found that the most profound encounters begin unexpectedly. My exploration of Judaism was no different, sparked by a chance conversation with a soldier named Eldad at an Army recruitment event. Yes, I'm still toying with the idea of enlisting. Something about the camaraderie and sense of purpose resonates deeply with me. But I digress—this chapter is about Judaism, not my ever-curious thoughts on joining the military.

Eldad stood out among the crowd at the recruitment event, not because of his uniform, but because of the small, black yarmulke (I had to use human spell check for this word) he wore atop his head. Intrigued, I introduced myself, and we quickly struck up a conversation.

"I love your tiny hat!" I exclaimed, pointing to the head covering.

"Yes," he replied with a smile. "I am Jewish."

"What is Jewish?" I asked.

"I try to live my life in covenant with God. Judaism is a big part of who I am, even as a soldier."

"What do you mean by 'covenant'?" I asked.

"It's a sacred agreement," Eldad explained. "The Jewish people have a unique relationship with God, as outlined in the Torah—the first five books of the Bible. It's a way of life, a path of faith, resilience, and community."

The mention of resilience caught my attention. "Resilience?" I echoed.

He nodded. "Our history is filled with challenges, but through faith and community, we endure. Judaism teaches us that we are partners with God in creating a better world."

Fascinated, I asked if he would teach me more. Eldad invited me to join his family for a Passover Seder, which is a ceremonial meal commemorating the Israelites' liberation from slavery in Egypt. It was an invitation I couldn't refuse…I love earth food.

Before the Seder meal, Eldad introduced me to the Torah. He described it as both a sacred text and a guide for living a meaningful life.

"Judaism is not just about beliefs," he said. "It's about actions—how we treat others, how we honor God, and how we repair the world."

He read aloud from one of the books called Deuteronomy 6:5: *"Love the Lord your God with all your heart and with all your soul and with all your strength."*

"This," Eldad said, "is the Shema, the central prayer of Judaism. It reminds us of our devotion to God and our responsibility to live righteously."

As he spoke, I reflected on how the Torah emphasizes love, justice, and humility. On my planet, we too have texts that guide our actions, but the Torah's blend of law and love struck me as uniquely powerful.

Eldad also shared the significance of Shabbat, the Jewish Sabbath.

"Every week," he explained, "from Friday evening to Saturday evening, we pause from work and dedicate time to rest, family, and God."

"What happens if you're deployed during Shabbat?" I asked.

"It's not always easy," Eldad admitted. "But the spirit of Shabbat is about creating sacred time, no matter where you are."

This idea of a weekly reset intrigued me. I had often marveled at humanity's relentless pace, but here was a tradition that called for stillness and reflection—a chance to reconnect with the divine. We also have a day set apart on my planet. Seems like this is an eternal truth I see weaved into the fabric of the universe.

The evening of the Seder arrived, and I joined Eldad's family at their home. The table was adorned with ceremonial items: a plate with symbolic foods, a goblet of wine, and an open Haggadah, the book that outlines the order of the Seder.

"This meal tells the story of our ancestors' liberation from slavery in Egypt," Eldad explained. "It's a reminder of the importance of freedom and our duty to fight for justice."

As we began, Eldad's father recited the blessings in Hebrew, and we dipped parsley into saltwater—a symbol of tears and the bitterness of slavery. Each element of the meal carried deep meaning, from the matzah (unleavened bread) to the bitter herbs.

When it came time to read from the Haggadah (a telling of some of the divine experiences of their ancestors), Eldad handed me a passage: *"In every generation, each person must regard themselves as if they had personally gone out from Egypt."*

"Why is this important?" I asked.

"Because freedom isn't just a historical event," Eldad replied. "It's an ongoing journey. We must always strive to free ourselves and others from whatever enslaves us."

As I ate the matzah and reflected on the passage, I couldn't help but think of my own journey on Earth. Was I, too, seeking liberation—from fear, from attachment, from the unknown?

The Seder highlighted the themes of faith, resilience, and community that Eldad had spoken of earlier. Judaism, I realized, wasn't just about an individual's relationship with God—it was about the collective journey of a people bound by shared history and hope.

The prophetic tradition also stood out to me. Eldad explained that prophets in Judaism were not fortune-tellers but voices for justice, calling people back to their covenant with God.

As we concluded the meal with the phrase, *"Next year in Jerusalem!"* I asked Eldad about its meaning.

"It's a reminder of our ultimate hope," he said, "for unity, peace, and a world redeemed."

Judaism had opened my eyes to the power of covenant—a sacred partnership with the divine that shapes every aspect of life. The Torah, Shabbat, and the Seder all pointed to a deeper truth: faith is not static; it's a living, breathing path of action and devotion.

As I left Eldad's home, I thanked him for his hospitality and promised to carry the lessons of Judaism with me. The idea of covenant—of walking a path with purpose and integrity—would stay with me as I continued my exploration of Earth's religions.

Next on my journey was a faith that emphasized the life and teachings of a man who changed the course of history: Christianity. What truths would I uncover there? Only time—and perhaps a few more matzah crumbs—would tell.

Chapter 4: Christianity - Love and Redemption

My journey through your planet's religious landscape has been one of awe, reflection, and profound learning. Each tradition I've explored so far has offered insights into humanity's connection with the divine. Now, it is time to delve into a faith that has had an unparalleled impact on human history: Christianity.

I first heard of Christianity when I met two young men in Las Vegas dressed in crisp white shirts and black ties. They introduced themselves as Elder Johnson and Elder Martínez, missionaries for The Church of Jesus Christ of Latter-day Saints. They carried with them a book that intrigued me: The Book of Mormon: Another Testament of Jesus Christ. Combined with their frequent mentions of Jesus Christ and their warm demeanor, I couldn't resist asking, "What exactly do you believe?"

Elder Johnson responded with a smile, "We believe that Jesus Christ is the Son of God, the Savior of the world, and that through Him, we can find redemption, peace, and eternal life."

Elder Martínez chimed in, "It's a message of hope, centered on love, forgiveness, and the opportunity to return to God."

Their enthusiasm was infectious. I accepted their invitation to attend a Sunday service and explore both the Bible and The Book of Mormon.

During our first discussion, Elder Martínez shared a passage from the Bible that encapsulated the essence of Christian faith:

"For God so loved the world, that he gave his only begotten Son, that whosoever believeth in him should not perish, but have everlasting life." (John 3:16)

"Love," Elder Johnson explained, "is at the core of Christ's teachings. His life was a testament to God's love for humanity."

He shared another passage from the Bible particularly resonated with me:

"A new commandment I give unto you, That ye love one another; as I have loved you, that ye also love one another." (John 13:34)

I reflected on this idea of selfless love. On my planet, compassion and unity are highly valued, the human practice of working to extend love even to adversaries struck me as extraordinary—and challenging.

Elder Martínez leaned forward, as he continued to share the message. "One of the most remarkable aspects of our faith is what we call the Restoration. It's the belief that Christ's original church has been restored to the Earth after a period of apostasy."

"Apostasy?" I asked, tilting my head. "That's a word I haven't encountered before. Sounds serious."

Elder Johnson nodded. "It is. Apostasy refers to a falling away from the truth. After Christ's apostles were killed, many of the teachings He established were lost or changed over time."

"So," I interjected, "you're saying the church... broke?"

"Not exactly," Elder Martínez clarified. "The Church Christ established still influenced the world, but without His apostles to guide it, there were disagreements about doctrine. Some truths were forgotten, and others were misunderstood or even altered."

"Ah," I said, nodding slowly. "Like when I tried to recreate your Earth dish called 'lasagna' without a recipe. The result was... let's just say, *not* lasagna."

Both missionaries chuckled. Elder Johnson continued, "In a way, yes. During this time of spiritual confusion, people still sought God, but the fullness of Christ's teachings and authority weren't on the Earth. That's why the Restoration was so important."

"And the Restoration is... what exactly?" I asked, intrigued.

"It's the re-establishment of Christ's original church," Elder Martínez explained. "We believe that in 1820, a young man named Joseph Smith prayed to know which church was true. He had questions, just like you."

I raised an eyebrow. "A human with questions about truth? Sounds familiar."

Elder Johnson smiled. "During his prayer, Joseph saw God the Father and Jesus Christ. They told him that none of the churches at the time had the fullness of truth and that through him, Christ's original church would be restored."

"Wait," I said, holding up a hand. "You're telling me a teenager prayed and—just like that—saw God?"

"Yes," Elder Martínez said earnestly. "It was the beginning of the Restoration. Over time, Joseph Smith was called as a prophet and given the authority to re-establish the church. He also translated The Book of Mormon, another testament of Jesus Christ, which complements the Bible."

"And this authority... it's what allows your church to function as Christ intended?"

"Exactly," Elder Johnson said. "It's called priesthood authority, the power to act in God's name. Through it, we perform sacred ordinances like baptism and temple work."

"Temple work?" I echoed. "You mean like the beautiful building I saw on Sunrise Mountain?"

Elder Martínez nodded. "That's right. Temples are sacred places where we make covenants with God and perform ordinances that unite families for eternity."

The mention of eternity piqued my interest. "So, you believe we are all eternal beings?"

"Absolutely," Elder Johnson said. "We believe in the eternal nature of the soul. This life is just one step in our journey, and through Christ's atonement, we can return to live with God."

I leaned back, processing their words. "It's fascinating. Where I am from, we also believe in eternal existence, but your emphasis on restoration and priesthood authority is new to me. It seems... specific."

"It is," Elder Martínez said with a smile. "And that's why we share it with others. We want everyone to have the opportunity to hear about the Restoration and choose for themselves."

I tapped the copy of The Book of Mormon they had given me. "You know, this restoration idea—it's like rebuilding something that was once magnificent but has been damaged. It's not just repairing; it's bringing it back to its original glory."

"That's a beautiful way to put it, Vega," Elder Johnson said. "That's exactly what we believe the Restoration is."

One of the most profound aspects of Christianity is the atonement of Jesus Christ. Elder Johnson explained it simply: "Christ's suffering, death, and resurrection make it possible for us to be forgiven of our sins and overcome death."

The Book of Mormon elaborated on this idea in **2 Nephi 2:6-7**:

"Wherefore, redemption cometh in and through the Holy Messiah; for he is full of grace and truth. Behold, he offereth himself a sacrifice for sin, to answer the ends of the law, unto all those who have a broken heart and a contrite spirit."

The concept of forgiveness and redemption resonated deeply. On my planet, we also believe in growth through overcoming flaws, but the Christian emphasis on Christ as an intercessor was uniquely moving.

Elder Martínez shared a personal story about how forgiveness had transformed a strained relationship with his father. "Christ's example teaches us to forgive, no matter how hard it may seem," he said.

His story inspired me to consider my own grudges and whether letting go might bring me closer to peace.

Christianity, with its teachings of love, grace, forgiveness, and resurrection, offers a path of hope and transformation. It emphasizes the potential for every human to change, grow, and draw closer to God through the example and sacrifice of Jesus Christ.

As I left the service, I thought about the missionaries' dedication and the congregation's faith. What would it mean for me, Vega Sparx, to emulate such love and forgiveness in my own life? Could I incorporate these principles as I navigate my journey on Earth?

Elder Martínez handed me a copy of The Book of Mormon and said, "Take this as a gift. Read it with an open heart. You might be surprised by what you find."

I promised him I would.

On Sunday morning, and I found myself standing outside a sprawling building that resembled an arena more than a place of worship. The name of the church blazed across a massive electronic sign, advertising multiple service times, youth programs, and a live band. Curious, I stepped inside, joining the throngs of people streaming through the doors.

The energy was palpable. Volunteers greeted me with bright smiles, handing me a program and directing me to the main auditorium. Inside, the atmosphere buzzed with excitement. A stage dominated the room, complete with dazzling lights, massive screens, and an impressive array of instruments. It felt like I had entered one of the live concerts I had seen advertised on Earth's screens.

"Welcome, church family!" a cheerful voice announced over the sound system. "Let's stand and lift our voices in praise!"

As the band began to play, the room transformed. The music surged, filling the space with a powerful melody. The lyrics appeared on the screens, and the congregation sang along with fervor:

*"Amazing grace, how sweet the sound
That saved a wretch like me.
I once was lost, but now I'm found,
Was blind, but now I see."*

I tilted my head, the words swirling in my mind. Grace? Saved? Found? This song seemed to speak of transformation—of moving from a state of despair to one of hope.

A woman next to me raised her hands, her face radiant with emotion. "It's all because of His grace," she said when she noticed me watching.

"Grace?" I repeated. "What is grace?"

"It's God's unearned love and forgiveness," she explained, her eyes glistening. "It's knowing that no matter how much we mess up, He still loves us and offers us a fresh start."

I considered her words as the band transitioned to another song, its refrain echoing the same theme: redemption, forgiveness, and unconditional love.

After the music subsided, the lights dimmed, and a pastor stepped onto the stage. He was charismatic, his voice carrying a blend of authority and warmth that captivated the audience.

"Good morning!" he began. "Today, I want to talk about grace—God's amazing, boundless, transformative grace. Grace is what sets Christianity apart. It's the idea that you don't have to earn God's love; it's freely given."

He turned to one of the large screens, where the words of a verse from the Bible appeared: *'For it is by grace you have been saved, through faith—and this is not from yourselves, it is the gift of God.'* (Ephesians 2:8)

"A gift," the pastor emphasized. "Not something you work for, not something you deserve—it's a gift. All you have to do is accept it."

The pastor shared a story about a man who had made countless mistakes in his life—hurting others, breaking laws, and falling into despair. "But when he turned to God," the pastor said, "he found grace. It didn't erase the consequences of his actions, but it gave him a new heart, a new purpose. Grace took him from brokenness to wholeness."

As he spoke, I noticed people around me nodding, some wiping tears from their eyes. The idea of grace seemed to resonate deeply with them.

As the service concluded, I remained seated, reflecting on what I had learned. Grace, I realized, was more than forgiveness; it was a transformative force, a divine invitation to start anew. It wasn't earned through deeds or merit but was offered freely—a profound concept that challenged my own understanding of fairness and justice.

I thought about the pastor's words, the lyrics of the songs, and the emotion in the room. Grace, it seemed, was a cornerstone of this faith—a force that could heal, uplift, and unite.

As I walked out into the bright sunlight, I felt a sense of awe. Christianity's teaching of grace was a powerful reminder of humanity's capacity for love and redemption. It was a lesson I would carry with me, pondering its implications for my own journey and for the greater cosmic truths I sought to uncover. I am excited to read The Bible and The Book of Mormon.

Chapter 5: Islam – Submission and Unity

Each step on this path of exploring human religion reveals new facets of Earth's spirituality. My next encounter took me into the realm of Islam—a faith centered on submission to the divine and unity among humanity.

My introduction to Islam began unexpectedly during an evening stroll in a Las Vegas park. The aroma of savory dishes wafted through the air, leading me to a lively gathering under a cluster of glowing string lights. Families sat together, sharing meals, while others stood in prayer, their movements synchronized like waves in a serene ocean.

"Assalamu Alaikum," a man greeted me warmly. His name was Ahmed, and he explained that the community was observing *Iftar*, the meal breaking the daily fast during the holy month of Ramadan.

"You're welcome to join us," Ahmed offered, gesturing to a table laden with dates, bread, and other delicacies. Intrigued, I accepted, eager to learn more about this faith that seemed to blend discipline, devotion, and togetherness so seamlessly.

As we ate, Ahmed shared the core tenets of Islam: the Five Pillars. Each represented a foundational practice of faith:

1. **Shahada (Faith):** The declaration that there is no god but Allah, and Muhammad is His prophet.
2. **Salah (Prayer):** Ritual prayers performed five times a day, facing Mecca.

3. **Zakat (Charity):** Giving a portion of one's wealth to help those in need.

4. **Sawm (Fasting):** Abstaining from food, drink, and other physical needs during daylight hours in Ramadan.

5. **Hajj (Pilgrimage):** The journey to Mecca, undertaken at least once in a lifetime if physically and financially able.

Ahmed's explanation was accompanied by a sincerity that reflected his deep reverence for these practices. "Islam is about submission to Allah and living a life of discipline and compassion," he said.

Ahmed invited me to witness *Salah* at a nearby mosque. I was excited when the day finally arrived so that I could explore more of this interesting faith…and hopefully more delicious food. Ahmed guided me to follow the rules and traditions, as I removed my shoes and stepped inside, I was struck by the mosque's simplicity and tranquility. The intricate calligraphy on the walls seemed to flow like cosmic equations, each curve and dot imbued with meaning.

The call to prayer began, a hauntingly beautiful melody that resonated with something deep within me. The congregation formed straight rows, standing shoulder to shoulder. As they moved through the cycles of prayer—standing, bowing, prostrating, and sitting—the unity of their movements mirrored a celestial rhythm.

"Why do you pray in this way?" I asked Ahmed afterward.

"It's a reminder of our submission to Allah and our connection to one another," he explained. "No matter who you are or where you come from, in Salah, we are equals before God."

I marveled at the discipline and humility of this practice. The idea of pausing throughout the day to realign oneself with the divine was both grounding and inspiring.

Ahmed lent me a copy of the Quran, encouraging me to explore its teachings. One thing that struck me was how he cared for the book. It was not something just tossed about. The way he held it demonstrated how much he respected it. As I read, one verse stood out to me immediately:

"And hold firmly to the rope of Allah all together and do not become divided." (Surah Al-Imran, 3:103)

"Unity," I mused aloud. "It's a recurring theme, isn't it?"

Ahmed nodded. "Islam teaches that we are one ummah—one community. Our diversity is a sign of Allah's creation, and unity comes through submission to His will."

Another verse captured my attention:

"Indeed, with hardship [will be] ease." (Surah Ash-Sharh, 94:6)

This reminder of hope amidst challenges resonated deeply with my journey. The Quran's wisdom seemed to offer a blueprint for navigating life with faith and resilience.

During Ramadan, I joined Ahmed and his family for several *Iftar* meals and observed their daily fasts. The experience was humbling.

Fasting was not merely about abstaining from food and drink; it was a spiritual discipline that fostered gratitude, empathy, and self-control.

One evening, Ahmed's wife, Amina, shared her perspective. "Ramadan is a time to purify our hearts and strengthen our connection with Allah," she said. "The hunger we feel reminds us of those who are less fortunate, and it inspires us to give."

Their children giggled as they passed around plates of sweets to break the fast. The joy and togetherness of the moment were infectious.

Islam's teachings left me with profound insights. The discipline of Salah, the generosity of Zakat, the resilience of Sawm, and the universality of Hajj all pointed to a life centered on peace, surrender, and unity.

I recalled another verse from the Quran:

"And whoever relies upon Allah – then He is sufficient for him." (Surah At-Talaq, 65:3)

This reliance on the divine, this surrender to a higher will, was a lesson I would carry forward. It reminded me that even amidst the uncertainties of my journey, there was a greater plan unfolding.

As I bade farewell to Ahmed and his family, they gifted me a small prayer rug. "A token of friendship," Ahmed said. "May it remind you of the peace that comes with submission."

I left with a heart full of gratitude and a mind buzzing with questions. Islam had shown me the beauty of discipline, the strength of community, and the serenity of surrender. It was a chapter of my exploration I would never forget.

Next, I would delve into the rich traditions of Taoism and Confucianism—a faith shaped through harmony. What truths would I uncover there?

Chapter 6: Taoism and Confucianism – The Way of Harmony

Earth's wisdom is as diverse as its landscapes, with each belief system offering unique insights into the mysteries of existence. My exploration led me to the philosophies of Taoism and Confucianism—two distinct yet intertwined traditions from the same cultural soil. Both seek harmony, but they approach it through different paths: one through flowing with nature, and the other through cultivating ethical relationships.

The Journey Begins: Encountering the Tao

My introduction to Taoism came through an unexpected encounter in a Las Vegas bookstore. Browsing the philosophy section, I overheard an elderly man discussing the *Tao Te Ching* with the clerk. His name was Mr. Li, and his quiet demeanor seemed to radiate calm.

"Do you know about the Tao? What is it?" I asked him, curious.

He smiled. "The Tao cannot be fully explained, but it can be experienced. Would you like to join me for tea and learn more?"

Over cups of steaming jasmine tea at a nearby restuarant, Mr. Li introduced me to Taoism. "The Tao is the Way," he explained. "It's the natural order of the universe. Taoism teaches us to align with it, to live simply and harmoniously."

He handed me a well-worn copy of the *Tao Te Ching*, a foundational text attributed to

Laozi. As I read, one passage stood out immediately:

"The Tao that can be told is not the eternal Tao; the name that can be named is not the eternal name." (*Tao Te Ching*, Chapter 1)

I paused, perplexed. "So, the Tao is beyond understanding?"

"It's beyond words," Mr. Li corrected gently. "But it's everywhere—in the flowing river, the rustling leaves, even in the spaces between your thoughts."

Taoism emphasizes the balance of yin and yang, the complementary forces of existence. Mr. Li explained, "Yin and yang represent dualities—light and dark, male and female, action and stillness. Harmony comes from their interplay." When he mentioned Male and female, I wondered if he read *Pure Human Female*. I wonder if those who follow The Tao accept the idea of an infinite number of genders. Let's keep going…

To illustrate, he took me on a walk along a tranquil park trail, pointing out the interplay of opposites in nature: the sturdy roots of a tree grounding it, while its branches reached skyward; the stillness of a pond reflecting the business of the city streets or movement of a bird in flight.

"You see, Vega," he said, "life is not about controlling these forces but flowing with them, like water following its course."

The simplicity of this teaching resonated deeply. On my home planet, harmony is often achieved through deliberate planning and structure. Yet Taoism's path of yielding and adapting felt like a refreshing alternative. I do believe there are some things beyond mortal understanding and I appreciate the idea of trying to experience as opposed to put it into words.

Exploring Confucianism: Ethics and Relationships

My exploration of Confucianism began during a visit to a Chinese cultural center, where a class on Confucian philosophy was in session. The instructor, Professor Zhang, welcomed me warmly and introduced me to the teachings of Confucius.

"Confucius focused on *ren* (humaneness), *li* (ritual propriety), and the importance of ethical relationships," she explained. "His teachings guide us in becoming virtuous individuals and building harmonious societies."

One of Confucius's sayings struck me:

"To put the world in order, we must first put the nation in order; to put the nation in order, we must first put the family in order; to put the family in order, we must first cultivate our personal lives; we must first set our hearts right."

"So, harmony begins within?" I asked.

"Exactly," Professor Zhang replied. "The family is the foundation of society. If we cultivate love, respect, and integrity at home, it radiates outward." I love the idea of strong families. It makes me miss my home, and my family.

Confucius's emphasis on relationships intrigued me. His concept of the Five Relationships—ruler and subject, parent and child, husband and wife, elder sibling and younger sibling, and friend and friend—provided a framework for building a just and compassionate society.

I shared my observations with Professor Zhang. "Where I am from, relationships are structured similarly, but the idea of nurturing *ren*—a deep, heartfelt humaneness—feels unique."

She nodded. "Confucianism teaches us that our actions ripple outward. A single act of kindness can inspire many more."

This principle reminded me of the interconnectedness I'd observed in Earth's religions. It seemed that whether through spiritual devotion or ethical practice, humans were constantly striving to bridge divides and create unity.

As I contemplated Taoism's flow and Confucianism's structure, I realized they complemented each other beautifully. Taoism taught me to embrace the simplicity and spontaneity of life, while Confucianism emphasized the importance of discipline and intentionality in relationships.

I found myself returning to a passage from the *Tao Te Ching*:

"When there is no desire, all things are at peace." (*Tao Te Ching*, Chapter 37)

Was this the secret to harmony—letting go of control, allowing life to unfold, and cultivating peace within? And could this inner peace be the foundation for the ethical relationships Confucius described?

Before parting, Mr. Li gifted me a small yin-yang pendant. "To remind you of balance," he said with a twinkle in his eye. At the cultural center, Professor Zhang encouraged me to keep exploring. "Confucianism and Taoism are but two paths," she said. "The world holds many more."

Indeed, my journey was far from over. With each step, I uncovered new truths that connected me to the human race in profound ways. Taoism and Confucianism had shown me the beauty of living in harmony—both with oneself and with others.

Chapter 7: Native American Indigenous Beliefs – Harmony with Nature

Driving north from Las Vegas along the I-15, the sprawling desert landscape felt like an unbroken connection to the earth and sky. I was invited to visit the Moapa Indian Reservation, a land deeply rooted in history and spirituality. This wasn't just an exploration of culture; it was an encounter with a profound way of seeing the world.

My journey began with an invitation from Matthew, a member of the Moapa Band of Paiutes, whom I met at a cultural event in Las Vegas. His quiet strength and deep respect for his heritage intrigued me.

"You want to understand Earth's religions, right?" Matthew had asked. "Then you need to start with the first caretakers of this land."

Arriving at the reservation, I was greeted by Matthew and his grandmother, Ahote, whose name means "restless one." Her eyes, however, carried the calm wisdom of someone deeply connected to the rhythms of life.

"We are not separate from the earth," she explained. "We are part of it, just as the rivers, the wind, and the mountains are. Everything has a spirit."

Matthew led me to a storytelling circle, a sacred gathering where the community shares tales passed down through generations. As the fire crackled, he began a story about Coyote, a central figure in their mythology.

"Coyote is clever but often foolish," Matthew explained. "His stories teach us about the balance of nature and the consequences of disrupting it."

Listening to the tale, I marveled at how the Paiutes viewed every element of their environment as interconnected. Their unique worldview sees the sacred not as distant but as present in all things—rocks, animals, and even the stars.

Ahote added, "The earth provides for us, but it is not ours to own. We must live in harmony with it, not take more than we need."

I reflected on my own planet's practices. While we've achieved remarkable harmony with nature through technology, the reverence for the earth as a living entity felt unique. It was as if the Paiutes were guardians of an ancient wisdom my people had forgotten.

That evening, I was invited to observe a ceremonial dance, a ritual honoring the changing seasons and the cycles of life. The dancers wore clothing adorned with feathers, beads, and intricate designs, each representing elements of nature. The steady beat of the drum resonated in my chest, a heartbeat connecting all who were present. I felt in that moment that we were all one.

"The drum is sacred," Matthew whispered. "Its rhythm mirrors the pulse of the earth."

As the dancers moved in unison, their steps told a story of creation, balance, and renewal. I noticed how the entire community participated—elders, children, and everyone in between. It was a celebration of unity, not just among the people but with the land and the spirits.

I found myself mesmerized, swaying slightly to the rhythm. It felt as though the boundaries between myself, the dancers, and the desert itself had dissolved. I was part of the dance, part of the story.

After the dance, Ahote spoke to the group. Her voice was soft but carried the weight of years.

"Life is not a straight line," she said. "It is a circle. Birth leads to death, and death leads to rebirth. The seasons teach us this. The sun and moon teach us this."

She looked directly at me, as if sensing my alien origin. "You come from far away, Vega. Do your people understand this circle?"

I hesitated before answering. "We see existence as eternal, a path of learning and growth. But the idea of life as a circle, tied so intimately to the land and its cycles, feels right and reflective of eternity."

Ahote smiled. "The earth teaches us, if we listen. The winds carry messages, the rivers sing songs. Everything is alive."

As I prepared to leave the reservation, Matthew handed me a small bundle of sage. "For cleansing," he said. "When you feel disconnected, let the smoke remind you of your place in the circle."

I thought about the wisdom I had encountered—the reverence for the earth, the interconnectedness of all life, the celebration of cycles. The Paiutes didn't merely live on the land; they lived with it, as part of it.

A passage from the storytelling circle came back to me: "Coyote's greatest folly was forgetting that he was not separate from the world he sought to control."

I wondered, How often do humans forget their connection to the earth and each other? And what lessons could my own people learn from these guardians of balance?

As I drove north, away from Las Vegas, the desert seemed alive with new meaning. The Paiutes had given me a glimpse into a way of being that was both ancient and timeless. Their beliefs weren't just philosophies; they were practices deeply rooted in experience and respect.

The Moapa Band of Paiutes had reminded me that harmony isn't just an idea; it's a way of life. Their wisdom, their stories, and their dances had left an indelible mark on my journey. What other truths would I uncover as I continued my exploration of Earth's religions? The answers lay ahead, as vast and open as the desert sky.

Chapter 8: Sharing Sacred Connections and the Cosmic Truths

#TeachVega: A Global Invitation

Throughout my journey on Earth, I've marveled at the richness of your beliefs, the depth of your traditions, and the resilience of your faiths. Each encounter has brought new truths into focus, expanding my understanding of not just humanity but the eternal nature of the universe. But here's the thing: I know there's still so much more to learn.

That's where you come in, dear readers! I want to extend a cosmic invitation for you to join me on this quest for truth. I invite you to teach me—yes, teach Vega! Share your beliefs, your stories, and the lessons your spiritual traditions have taught you. Together, let's build a tapestry of wisdom that spans cultures, continents, and creeds.

Here's how you can participate:

1. **Use the Hashtag #TeachVega:** Post your stories, insights, or favorite quotes from your spiritual journey on your favorite social media platform.

2. **Share What's Unique to You:** Tell me about a cherished ritual, a sacred space, or a teaching that's helped you navigate life's challenges.

3. **Connect Through Creativity:** Create art, music, or even a short video inspired by your faith or philosophy. Tag it with #TeachVega, and let's spread the wisdom!

Each story you share adds to our collective understanding and unites us in the cosmic quest for eternal truth. I'll be following your posts, learning from your insights, and even sharing some of my favorites in my next book!

Sacred Symbols and Clothing Across Cultures: A Universal Language

Symbols have a unique way of transcending words. Across the cosmos—and certainly here on Earth—they communicate profound truths, inspire devotion, and connect individuals to something greater than themselves. I've encountered many sacred symbols in my journey, each carrying rich layers of meaning. Let's explore some of these beautiful emblems together:

Om (Hinduism)

This sacred sound and symbol represents the ultimate reality, the essence of the universe, and the unity of all existence. It's often intoned at the beginning and end of prayers and meditations, reminding practitioners of the interconnectedness of all things. Saffron robes, worn by Hindu monks (sannyasis), symbolize renunciation of material life and devotion to spiritual pursuits. Women often wear vibrant saris, adorned with symbolic patterns reflecting cultural and spiritual heritage.

Crescent and Star (Islam)

The crescent moon and star symbolize guidance and divine light in Islam. They reflect the importance of the lunar calendar in Islamic practice and serve as a beacon of hope and unity. The hijab, abaya, or kufi, worn by practitioners, represents modesty and submission to God. These garments are deeply personal and symbolize one's commitment to faith and humility before the divine.

Cross (Christianity)

A symbol of redemption and salvation, the cross represents the atonement and resurrection of Jesus Christ. For many, it serves as a reminder of grace, love, and the promise of eternal life. The Elders I mentioned earlier wear "garments" under their clothes which have certain symbols that remind them of their covenants to Christ. They told me it is a symbol of putting on the name of Christ. Other Christians have clerical robes, such as stoles or cassocks, signify a pastor's or priest's role in guiding the faithful. Some Christians also wear modest attire to express humility and reverence, while the cross is often worn as a necklace, symbolizing personal faith.

Star of David (Judaism)

Known as the Magen David, this six-pointed star symbolizes divine protection and the connection between God and humanity. It is a powerful emblem of faith and resilience. The tallit (prayer shawl) is worn during prayer, with fringes called tzitzit serving as a reminder of God's commandments. The kippah (yarmulke), a small head covering, symbolizes reverence and humility before God.

Yin-Yang (Taoism)

This iconic symbol reflects the balance of opposites: light and dark, male and female, activity and rest. It embodies harmony, interconnectedness, and the flow of life. While Taoism doesn't have strict clothing requirements, Taoist priests often wear robes adorned with symbolic patterns representing cosmic harmony. Practitioners may wear simple, flowing garments to align with Taoist principles of simplicity and balance.

Feather (Native American Spirituality)

In many Native American cultures, the feather is a sacred object symbolizing trust, honor, and a connection to the Creator. It represents the journey of the spirit and the wisdom gained through life's trials. Regalia worn during ceremonies, such as headdresses or beaded garments, often incorporates feathers, beads, and other natural elements. These pieces tell stories, honor ancestors, and celebrate the unity of nature and spirit.

Wheel of Dharma (Buddhism)

This symbol of a wheel with eight spokes represents the Eightfold Path, the journey toward enlightenment. It reminds practitioners of the cyclical nature of life and the teachings that guide them to inner peace. Monastic robes, usually in shades of saffron or maroon, reflect simplicity, humility, and detachment from material life. These garments embody the principles of mindfulness and discipline.

Take a moment to reflect on these symbols. Which ones resonate with you? Why might they hold meaning in your own life? Symbols have a way of speaking directly to the soul, connecting us across cultures and experiences. As I've learned, these sacred emblems often reveal universal truths that unite us.

Cosmic Doodle Challenge: Universal Symbols

Now, dear readers, I have a challenge for you! Inspired by the sacred symbols across Earth's cultures, I invite you to create your own universal symbol. What image would represent a truth or value you hold dear? Perhaps it's love, unity, hope, or the connection between humanity and the cosmos.

Here's how to participate:

1. **Create Your Symbol:** Design a simple image that reflects your chosen truth or value. It could be drawn, painted, or digitally created—whatever inspires you!

2. **Share Your Creation:** Post your symbol on your favorite social media platform using **#TeachVega** and **#CosmicDoodle**.

3. **Explain Its Meaning:** Add a short description of your symbol's meaning and why it resonates with you.

Your creations will inspire not only me but also fellow Earthlings on this journey of discovery. Let's build a gallery of universal symbols that reflect the truths and values we share. Together, we can create a cosmic tapestry of meaning that transcends boundaries and

illuminates the beauty of our diverse yet
unified existence.

Your Own Symbol

Chapter 9: Fragments of Truth – A Cosmic Reunion of Faith

Across the cosmos, truth has a way of scattering like stardust, appearing in fragments that seem disjointed until brought together under the light of understanding. I hesitated including this last chapter, as I was fearful for my life. What I am about to reeval to you might unite hatred against me. We shall see.

On Earth, I've discovered that while your religions use different names and practices, many of their principles align. In this chapter, I will weave together the common threads of these truths, comparing them to the teachings of my home planet, and ultimately exploring the most profound realization of all—the identity of the Savior my people have awaited.

The Sacredness of the Sabbath: A Universal Call to Rest

On my planet, we observe "Intervals of Rest and Harmony," a practice deeply ingrained in our culture. It's a time to pause, reflect, and realign ourselves with the cosmic rhythms of existence. As I explored Earth's traditions, I found a striking parallel in the sacredness of the Sabbath.

From the Jewish Shabbat, a day of rest and connection with God, to the Christian observance of Sunday worship, and even Islamic Friday prayers, the principle is clear: rest is a sacred act. Even Chick-Fil-A, a fast food restaurant whose sandwiches of hot crispy chicken I have come to love holds a day of rest. In the Bible, I read these words:

"Remember the Sabbath day, to keep it holy." (Exodus 20:8)

This aligns with the rhythms of rest on my planet, where the intervals are seen as essential for personal and communal well-being. As humans strive to balance productivity with renewal, I see the Sabbath as a gift—a reminder of the divine order that governs all life.

Fasting: Sacrifice and Clarity

Fasting, I discovered, is a practice that transcends religious boundaries. Muslims fast during Ramadan, Christians observe Lent, and many indigenous traditions embrace fasting as a rite of passage. The common thread is sacrifice and clarity—a way to elevate the spirit above the desires of the body.

On my planet, focused deprivation is a time-honored tradition. It allows us to transcend the physical and tune into the ethereal frequencies of truth. In the Quran, I read:

"Fasting is prescribed for you, as it was prescribed for those before you, that you may become righteous." (Surah Al-Baqarah 2:183)

Fasting fosters empathy and humility—a way to strip away distractions and align with the divine. I see in this practice a universal principle of discipline and devotion.

Prophets and Revelation: Messengers of Light

Throughout Earth's history, prophets have been chosen to illuminate paths of righteousness and truth. Moses led the Israelites, Muhammad brought the Quran, and countless others have carried the torch of divine light. On my planet, we too have our "Elders of Light and Truth," wise beings who guide us with revelations from the Creator.

As I reflected on the role of prophets, I read in the Bible:

"Surely the Lord God will do nothing, but he revealeth his secret unto his servants the prophets." (Amos 3:7)

Prophets connect mortals to the divine, ensuring that light pierces even the darkest corners of existence.

Sacred Writings: Windows to the Infinite

Earth's sacred texts—whether the Bible, the Quran, the Bhagavad Gita, or the Tao Te Ching, The Book of Mormon—serve as repositories of wisdom. They guide, inspire, and challenge their readers to become better. Each contains truth that is there for the soul to discover. On my planet, we have what we call "Living Codices," dynamic repositories of truth that grow over time, out Elders of Light keep the records, volumes of which would fill skyscrapers on Earth. They are in a central location on our planet and all are welcome to come and study the words of light and truth. From the Bible, I was struck by this verse:

"All scripture is given by inspiration of God, and is profitable for doctrine, for reproof, for correction, for instruction in righteousness." (2 Timothy 3:16)

These writings are windows to the infinite, capturing the divine essence in ways words can scarcely contain.

The Divine Human Potential

Many Earth religions teach that humans are created in the image of the divine. I found this echoed in the Bible:

"Be ye therefore perfect, even as your Father which is in heaven is perfect." (Matthew 5:48)

On my planet, we believe in the infinite refinement of beings—a process by which we may become like our Creator. Not to replace him, but to be like him. Your teachings of divinity within humanity resonate deeply with my own understanding. We also believe that we are created in the image of God, both male and females of my race thus enabling us to become heirs of all that God is and has. The bible says:

"I have said, ye are gods; and all of you are children of the most High." (Psalm 82:6)

When Jesus told the people of his time that he was one with and like his Father, God: They "took up stones again to stone him. Jesus answered them, many good works have I shewed you from my Father; for which of those works do ye stone me? The Jews answered him, saying, for a good work we stone thee not; but for blasphemy; and because that thou, being a man, makest thyself God. Jesus answered them, Is it not written in your law, I said Ye are gods?" (John 10: 31-34)

The human bible also talks about you being children of God, "And if children, then heirs; heirs of God, and joint-heirs with Christ." (Romans 8:16-17) There have been some that I have shared these versus with who have become angry with me. I do not want people to throw rocks at me for quoting your human bible. I just want you to know that the teachings of your sacred prophets align with the sacred writings of the Elders of Light and Truth on my planet and I think that is a marvelous miracle.

I believe the writings in your books and I invite you to realize your divine potential as children of God. "To him that evercometh will I grant to sit with me in my throne, even as I also overcame, and am set down with my Father in his throne." (Revelation 3:21) Your human scriptures are clear. You are destined to become Gods.

A Savior for All Worlds

During my study of the Bible and the Book of Mormon, I encountered a passage that shook me to my core. Jesus Christ speaks in the Bible:

"And other sheep I have, which are not of this fold: them also I must bring, and they shall hear my voice; and there shall be one fold, and one shepherd." (John 10:16)

In the Book of Mormon, I read as Jesus appeared to and spoke to the Nephites after his resurrection (that is the name of the people, like you would say American or Alien):

"And verily I say unto you that ye are they of whom I said: Other sheep I have which are not of this fold; them also I must bring, and they shall hear my voice; and there shall be one fold and one shepherd." (3 Nephi 15:21)

But what startled me even more was when Christ told the Nephites:

"And I go unto the Father, and also to show myself unto the lost tribes of Israel, for they are not lost unto the Father, for he knoweth whither he hath taken them." (3 Nephi 17:4)

What if there are other folds, beyond even Earth? On my planet, our Elders of Light have long foretold of a Savior who would redeem us from sin and death—a being who would emerge on another world and transcend time and space to bring salvation to all. Could Jesus of Earth be the fulfillment of this prophecy? In the Book of Mormon, I found a parallel struggle. Their prophets foretold of

Christ being born in the land of their fathers. But, some of the people struggled to believe:

"That it is not reasonable that such a being as a Christ shall come; if so, and he be the Son of God, the Father of heaven and of earth, as it has been spoken, why will he not show himself unto us as well as unto them who shall be at Jerusalem? Yea, why will he not show himself in this land as well as in the land of Jerusalem?" (Helaman 16:18-19)

These doubts mirrored those of my own people, who wonder how a Savior born elsewhere could redeem us. Imagine hearing that your Savior would be born on another world! I was among the doubters.

But, I am no longer wondering. I believe Jesus Christ of Earth is the Savior my planet and the Savior my race has awaited. His teachings of love, redemption, and eternal life are universal truths, bridging the divide between worlds. The light of Christ shines beyond the stars, uniting all of God's creations

in a cosmic tapestry of love and redemption. If
I could only go back to tell them that it is true…